GILBERT IN DEEP

Jane Clarke & Charles Fuge

SIMON AND SCHUSTER

London New York Sydney

Gilbert the Great White Shark loved
to play hide-and-seek with Rita Remora.

But they already knew all the nooks
and crannies in the coral reef,
and all the hiding places in the Wreck.

So one day after school, Gilbert asked his mother,
"Mum, can we go and play hide-and-seek
on the other side of the reef?"

"If you like," Mrs Munch smiled. "But be sure
to be back before the sun goes down.
And don't go over the Edge!"

Gilbert and Rita swam off happily.

The sea was rough on the other side of the reef.
When Gilbert hid in the surging surf,
Rita was tumbled and tossed by the waves.
And when Rita hid in the swirling seaweed,
Gilbert found it terribly tangly.

"I'm tired of playing hide-and-seek," sighed Gilbert.
"Let's swim off the Edge, and play hide-and-*deep!*"
"Your mum will be cross," warned Rita. "She'll go
off the deep end!"
"She won't know, as long as we're back before dark,"
grinned Gilbert.

The Edge of the reef dropped away into inky darkness.

"It's dark in the Deep," Gilbert said, peering over the Edge.
"You're not scared of the dark, are you?" asked Rita.
"Me? Scared?" gulped Gilbert.
"Great White Sharks aren't scared of *anything!*"

And they dived off the Edge together.

Above them, pale rays of watery sunshine
silhouetted a shimmering shadow.

"It's a ghost whale!" Rita froze in her fins.
"Boo!" Gilbert shouted.

The huge shadow broke up into glittering rainbows.
"It's only cuttlefish," he grinned.
"There's nothing to be scared of."

Down and down they dived through
the deep, dark ocean.

They stopped at the entrance to a cave.
"I can't see a thing in here!" said Gilbert. "It's the perfect
place to play hide-and-deep. My turn to hide!"
He took a deep breath and swam in.
Rita covered her eyes with her fins and began to count to ten.

Whump!
Gilbert bumped into an empty giant clamshell.
He wriggled inside. He closed his eyes
so he couldn't see how dark it was.

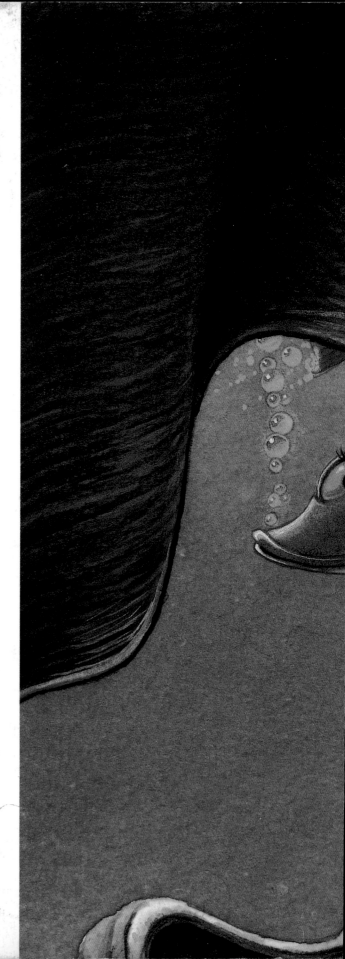

"8...9...10....
Ready or not, here I come!" Rita
called in a wobbly voice.

Gilbert opened one eye and peeked
out of the clamshell.

A ghostly green light was glowing
in the darkness.
The light bobbed closer.
Gilbert's heart beat faster.
The light bobbed past the clamshell.
It was bobbing towards Rita!

The light went out.

Gilbert's tummy did a somersault.
He squeezed out of his hiding
place. "R . . . R . . . Rita?
Where are you?"

"Gilbert!" Rita squealed.
"There's a green-eyed monster
in this cave!" Gilbert's teeth began
to chatter.

"I'm not a monster!" said a
gravelly voice indignantly. "I'm an
angler fish. My name is Glowanna."

"I . . . I can't see you," Gilbert
stammered. "It's much too dark."

"Why didn't you say so?" said
Glowanna. "All together now, cave.
Ready . . . Steady . . .

...glow!"

The cave was bathed in an eerie green light.
"Aargh!" Gilbert gasped.

"Aargh!" Glowanna and her friends
took one look at Gilbert's teeth and
leapt into each other's fins.

Rita crept back to Gilbert's side. Gilbert took a deep breath.
"H . . . hello, G . . . Glowanna," he spluttered.
"There's no need to be scared," said Glowanna.
"Me? Scared?" gulped Gilbert. "Great White Sharks
aren't scared of *anything!*"

Rita rolled her eyes.

"Uh-oh," she said. "The sun's going down. We'd better get back
before your mum finds out we went over the Edge."
"Let's go!" yelled Gilbert. "Come up and play
hide-and-seek with us sometime, Glowanna."
"I'm not going up there!" Glowanna gasped.
All sorts of scary things live in the light!"

Gilbert swam out of the cave.
"That's not the way we came!" called Rita.

But Gilbert was already swimming up
towards the rays of the setting sun.
Rita raced to catch him up.

All around them, seaweed was swaying and spooky shadows were swirling. Everything looked wrong.

"S-stick close to me, R-Rita," stammered Gilbert.

Moonlight began to filter into the deep blue ocean. Above them, a huge, silvery moonshadow was creeping along the Edge. A moonshadow with beady eyes and ferocious teeth. It crept closer, and closer, and . . .

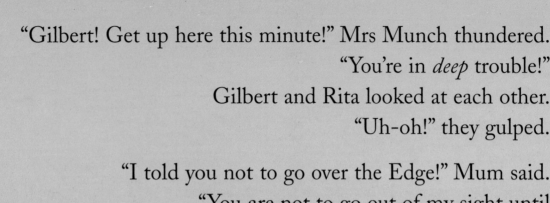

"Gilbert! Get up here this minute!" Mrs Munch thundered.
"You're in *deep* trouble!"
Gilbert and Rita looked at each other.
"Uh-oh!" they gulped.

"I told you not to go over the Edge!" Mum said.
"You are not to go out of my sight until
I am sure that I can trust you again!"

Gilbert's fins drooped. "S-s-sorry, Mum,"
he whispered. "We won't do it again!"

Mrs Munch hugged Gilbert tightly.
"Well, thank goodness I found you!
I was scared you were lost in the Deep," she said.
"I was a bit scared, too!" admitted Gilbert.

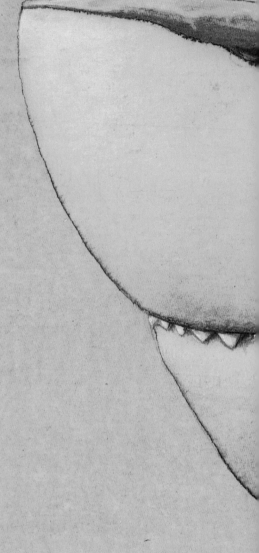

"You said Great White Sharks weren't afraid of *anything!*"
Rita reminded him.

In the moonlit ocean, Gilbert the Great White Shark
looked up at his mother and smiled a shaky, sharky smile.

"Well, *nearly* anything!" he grinned.

Fin